™

Hello, Fredbird!™

Ozzie Smith

Illustrated by M. De Angel with D. Moore

MASCOT BOOKS®
www.mascotbooks.com

It was a beautiful day in St. Louis.
Fredbird was on his way to the new Busch
Stadium for a St. Louis Cardinals game.

As Fredbird arrived at the stadium,
Cardinals fans cheered,
"Hello, Fredbird!"

Fredbird stopped at the
statue of Stan Musial,
one of the greatest players of all time.

As fans admired the statue,
they waved, "Hello, Fredbird!"

Fredbird watched batting practice.
The players wore their red jerseys
as they took practice swings.

The team's best hitter stepped to the plate and said, "Hello, Fredbird!"

After batting practice,
the Busch Stadium grounds crew
proudly prepared the field for play.

As the grounds crew worked,
they cheered, "Hello, Fredbird!"

Fredbird was hungry so he grabbed a
few snacks at the concession stand.

As he made his way back to the field,
a family cheered, "Hello, Fredbird!"

It was now time for player introductions and the National Anthem. Fredbird joined the team on the first base line.

Fredbird gazed at the American flag.
After the National Anthem,
the team said, "Hello, Fredbird!"

The umpire yelled, "PLAY BALL!"
and the first batter stepped to the plate.
It was time for the first pitch.

The Cardinals pitcher
delivered a perfect fastball.
The umpire called, "STRIKE ONE!"

Fredbird made his way into the
stands to visit with his friends.

His silly antics made everybody laugh.
Fans nearby cheered, "Hello, Fredbird!"

It was now time for the seventh inning
stretch. The organ played
"Take Me Out To The Ballgame!"™

Fredbird led the crowd
in song. Afterwards, Cardinals
fans cheered, "Hello, Fredbird!"

With the game tied in the
ninth inning, a Cardinals player hit
a deep fly ball. HOME RUN!

A lucky fan caught the ball.
The crowd cheered,
"Cardinals win, Fredbird!"

After the game, Fredbird headed home.
It had been a long day at the stadium.

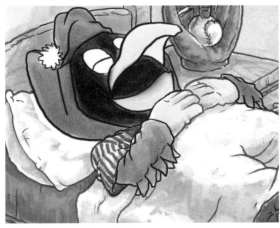

Fredbird was tired and fell fast asleep.
Good night, Fredbird!

For all the young Cardinals fans out there. ~ Ozzie Smith

For Sue, Ana Milagros, and Angel Miguel. ~ Miguel De Angel

Cardinals Care

Cardinals Care is the team's community foundation whose mission is caring for kids. For more information or to donate, contact:

Cardinals Care
100 S. 4th St., Suite 1200
St. Louis, MO 63102

Cardinals Crew

Join the greatest Kids' Club on earth, the Chevys Cardinals Crew Kids' Club! For more information, call 314-345-9600 or log on to: www.stlcardinals.com.

For more information about our products, please visit us online at www.mascotbooks.com.

Mascot Books, Inc.
P.O. Box 220157
Chantilly, VA 20153-0157

Major League Baseball trademarks and copyrights are used with permission of Major League Baseball Properties, Inc.

ISBN: 1-932888-83-7

PRT0610C

Printed in the United States

Baseball

Team	Title	Author
Boston Red Sox	Hello, *Wally*!	Jerry Remy
Boston Red Sox	*Wally The Green Monster* And His Journey Through *Red Sox Nation*!	Jerry Remy
Boston Red Sox	Coast to Coast with *Wally The Green Monster*	Jerry Remy
Boston Red Sox	A Season with *Wally The Green Monster*	Jerry Remy
Boston Red Sox	*Wally' The Green Monster* And His World Tour	Jerry Remy
Chicago Cubs	Let's Go, *Cubs*!	Aimee Aryal
Chicago White Sox	Let's Go, *White Sox*!	Aimee Aryal
Colorado Rockies	Hello, *Dinger*!	Aimee Aryal
Detroit Tigers	Hello, *Paws*!	Aimee Aryal
LA Angels	Let's Go, *Angels*!	Aimee Aryal
LA Dodgers	Let's Go, *Dodgers*!	Aimee Aryal
Milwaukee Brewers	Hello, *Bernie Brewer*!	Aimee Aryal
New York Yankees	Let's Go, *Yankees*!	Yogi Berra
New York Yankees	*Yankees* Town	Aimee Aryal
New York Mets	Hello, *Mr. Met*!	Rusty Staub
New York Mets	*Mr. Met* and his Journey Through the Big Apple	Aimee Aryal
Oakland Athletics	Let's Go, *A's*!	Aimee Aryal
Philadelphia Phillies	Hello, *Phillie Phanatic*!	Aimee Aryal
Cleveland Indians	Hello, *Slider*!	Bob Feller
San Francisco Giants	Go, *Giants*, Go!	Aimee Aryal
Seattle Mariners	Hello, *Mariner Moose*!	Aimee Aryal
St. Louis Cardinals	Hello, *Fredbird*!	Ozzie Smith
Washington Nationals	Hello, *Screech*!	Aimee Aryal

College

Team	Title	Author
Akron	Hello, Zippy	Jeremy Butler
Alabama	Hello, Big Al!	Aimee Aryal
Alabama	Roll Tide!	Ken Stabler
Alabama	Big Al's Journey Through the Yellowhammer State	Aimee Aryal
Arizona	Hello, Wilbur!	Lute Olson
Arizona State	Hello, Sparky!	Aimee Aryal
Arkansas	Hello, Big Red!	Aimee Aryal
Arkansas	Big Red's Journey Through the Razorback State	Aimee Aryal
Auburn	Hello, Aubie!	Aimee Aryal
Auburn	War Eagle!	Pat Dye
Auburn	Aubie's Journey Through the Yellowhammer State	Aimee Aryal
Boston College	Hello, Baldwin!	Aimee Aryal
Brigham Young	Hello, Cosmo!	LaVell Edwards
Cal - Berkeley	Hello, Oski!	Aimee Aryal
Cincinnati	Hello, Bearcat!	Mick Cronin
Clemson	Hello, Tiger!	Aimee Aryal
Clemson	Tiger's Journey Through the Palmetto State	Aimee Aryal
Colorado	Hello, Ralphie!	Aimee Aryal
Connecticut	Hello, Jonathan!	Aimee Aryal
Duke	Hello, Blue Devil!	Aimee Aryal
Florida	Hello, Albert!	Aimee Aryal
Florida	Albert's Journey Through the Sunshine State	Aimee Aryal
Florida State	Let's Go, 'Noles!	Aimee Aryal
Georgia	Hello, Hairy Dawg!	Aimee Aryal
Georgia	How 'Bout Them Dawgs!	Vince Dooley
Georgia	Hairy Dawg's Journey Through the Peach State	Vince Dooley
Georgia Tech	Hello, Buzz!	Aimee Aryal
Gonzaga	Spike, The Gonzaga Bulldog	Mike Pringle
Illinois	Let's Go, Illini!	Aimee Aryal
Indiana	Let's Go, Hoosiers!	Aimee Aryal
Iowa	Hello, Herky!	Aimee Aryal
Iowa State	Hello, Cy!	Amy DeLashmutt
James Madison	Hello, Duke Dog!	Aimee Aryal
Kansas	Hello, Big Jay!	Aimee Aryal
Kansas State	Hello, Willie!	Dan Walter
Kansas State	Willie the Wildcat's Journey Through the Sunflower State	Dan Walter
Kentucky	Hello, Wildcat!	Aimee Aryal
LSU	Hello, Mike!	Aimee Aryal
LSU	Mike's Journey Through the Bayou State	Aimee Aryal
Maryland	Hello, Testudo!	Aimee Aryal
Michigan	Let's Go, Blue!	Aimee Aryal
Michigan State	Hello, Sparty!	Aimee Aryal
Michigan State	Sparty's Journey Through Michigan	Aimee Aryal
Middle Tennessee	Hello, Lightning!	Aimee Aryal

Pro Football

Team	Title	Author
Carolina Panthers	Let's Go, Panthers!	Aimee Aryal
Chicago Bears	Let's Go, Bears!	Aimee Aryal
Dallas Cowboys	How 'Bout Them Cowboys!	Aimee Aryal
Green Bay Packers	Go, Pack, Go!	Aimee Aryal
Kansas City Chiefs	Let's Go, Chiefs!	Aimee Aryal
Minnesota Vikings	Let's Go, Vikings!	Aimee Aryal
New York Giants	Let's Go, Giants!	Aimee Aryal
New York Jets	J-E-T-S! Jets, Jets, Jets!	Aimee Aryal
New England Patriots	Let's Go, Patriots!	Aimee Aryal
Pittsburg Steelers	Here We Go, Steelers!	Aimee Aryal
Seattle Seahawks	Let's Go, Seahawks!	Aimee Aryal

Basketball

Team	Title	Author
Dallas Mavericks	Let's Go, Mavs!	Mark Cuban
Boston Celtics	Let's Go, Celtics!	Aimee Aryal

Other

	Title	Author
National	Bo America's Commander In Leash	Naren Aryal
Kentucky Derby	White Diamond Runs For The Roses	Aimee Aryal
Marine Corps Marathon	Run, Miles, Run!	Aimee Aryal

College (continued)

Team	Title	Author
Minnesota	Hello, Goldy!	Aimee Aryal
Mississippi	Hello, Colonel Rebel!	Aimee Aryal
Mississippi State	Hello, Bully!	Aimee Aryal
Missouri	Hello, Truman!	Todd Donoho
Missouri	Hello, Truman! Show Me Missouri!	Todd Donoho
Nebraska	Hello, Herbie Husker!	Aimee Aryal
North Carolina	Hello, Rameses!	Aimee Aryal
North Carolina	Rameses' Journey Through the Tar Heel State	Aimee Aryal
North Carolina St.	Hello, Mr. Wuf!	Aimee Aryal
North Carolina St.	Mr. Wuf's Journey Through North Carolina	Aimee Aryal
Northern Arizona	Hello, Louie!	Jeanette Baker
Notre Dame	Let's Go, Irish!	Aimee Aryal
Ohio State	Hello, Brutus!	Aimee Aryal
Ohio State	Brutus' Journey	Aimee Aryal
Oakland	Hello, Grizz!	Dawn Aubry
Oklahoma	Let's Go, Sooners!	Aimee Aryal
Oklahoma State	Hello, Pistol Pete!	Aimee Aryal
Oregon	Go Ducks!	Aimee Aryal
Oregon State	Hello, Benny the Beaver!	Aimee Aryal
Penn State	Hello, Nittany Lion!	Aimee Aryal
Penn State	We Are Penn State!	Joe Paterno
Purdue	Hello, Purdue Pete!	Aimee Aryal
Rutgers	Hello, Scarlet Knight!	Aimee Aryal
South Carolina	Hello, Cocky!	Aimee Aryal
South Carolina	Cocky's Journey Through the Palmetto State	Aimee Aryal
So. California	Hello, Tommy Trojan!	Aimee Aryal
Syracuse	Hello, Otto!	Aimee Aryal
Tennessee	Hello, Smokey!	Aimee Aryal
Tennessee	Smokey's Journey Through the Volunteer State	Aimee Aryal
Texas	Hello, Hook 'Em!	Aimee Aryal
Texas	Hook 'Em's Journey Through the Lone Star State	Aimee Aryal
Texas A & M	Howdy, Reveille!	Aimee Aryal
Texas A & M	Reveille's Journey Through the Lone Star State	Aimee Aryal
Texas Tech	Hello, Masked Rider!	Aimee Aryal
UCLA	Hello, Joe Bruin!	Aimee Aryal
Virginia	Hello, CavMan!	Aimee Aryal
Virginia Tech	Hello, Hokie Bird!	Aimee Aryal
Virginia Tech	Yea, It's Hokie Game Day!	Frank Beamer
Virginia Tech	Hokie Bird's Journey Through Virginia	Aimee Aryal
Wake Forest	Hello, Demon Deacon!	Aimee Aryal
Washington	Hello, Harry the Husky!	Aimee Aryal
Washington State	Hello, Butch!	Aimee Aryal
West Virginia	Hello, Mountaineer!	Aimee Aryal
West Virginia	The Mountaineer's Journey Through West Virginia	Leslie H. Haning
Wisconsin	Hello, Bucky!	Aimee Aryal
Wisconsin	Bucky's Journey Through the Badger State	Aimee Aryal